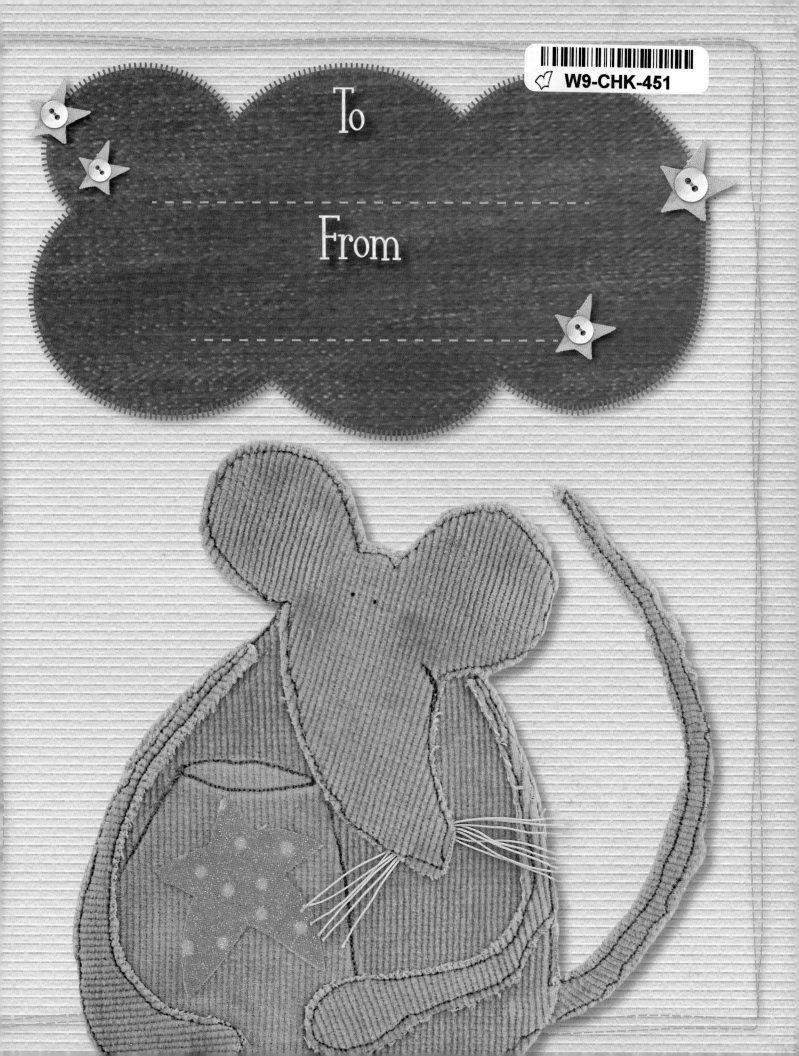

To

From

With thanks to Jane Horne

Copyright © 2007

make believe ideas

27 Castle Street, Berkhamsted,
Hertfordshire, HP4 2DW.

Manufactured in China

Twinkle, Twinkle, Little Star

Kate Toms

make believe ideas

Twinkle, twinkle,
little **star**,
How I wonder
what **you** are,

You **shine** above
the **world** so high,
Like a **lightbulb**
in the **sky**.

I'd love to catch you in my net...

And if the moon

Yummy!

is made of cheese,

14

Will you save some for me, please?

Twinkle, twinkle, little star,

What do you see from afar?

Hello

Hola!

Are there stars for us all up there?

All mine!

Wheeeeee!

18

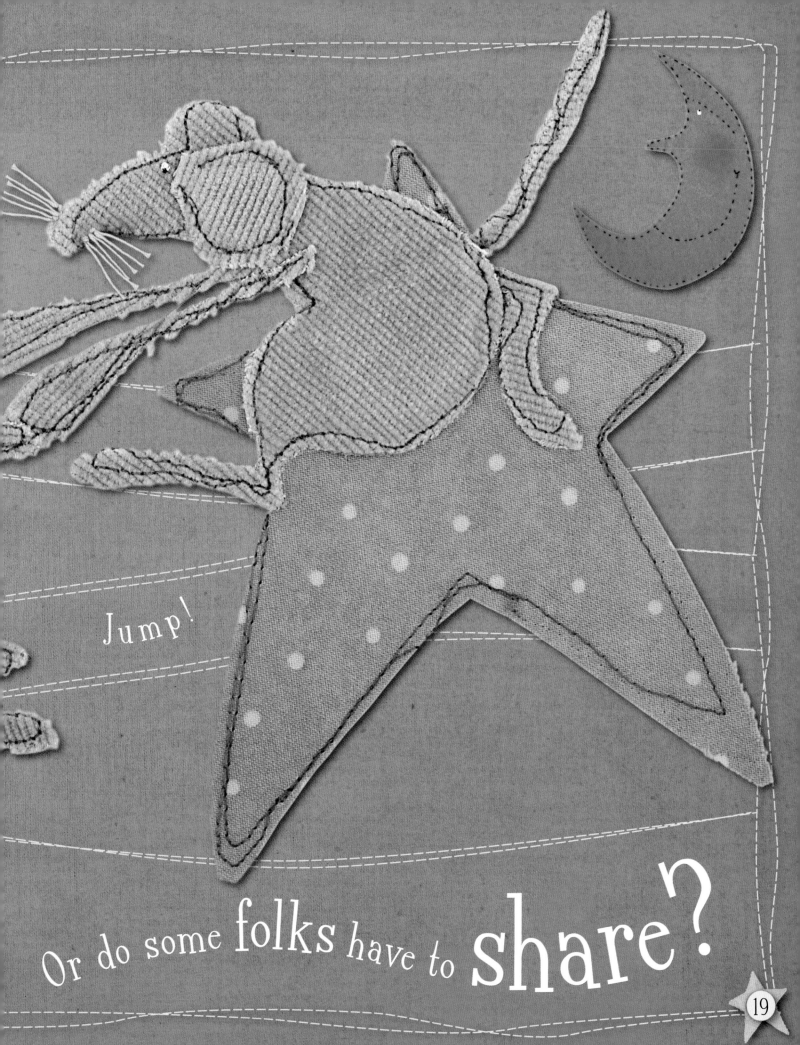

Jump!

Or do some folks have to share?

19

Twinkle, twinkle, little star,
How I wonder what you are!

When the sky grows dark at night,
I wish and wish with all my might,

That you would look down
on my **house,**
And grant one thing
for this small **mouse**.

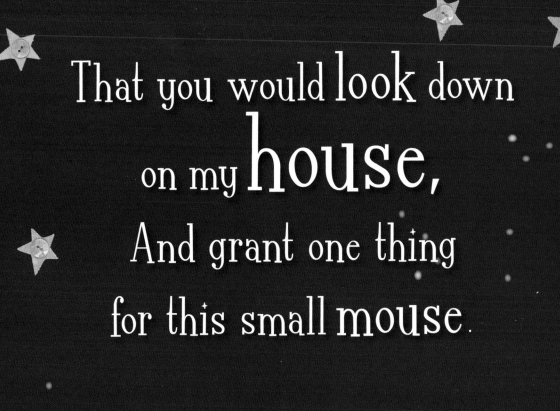

I want to be a **star** like you,

W h e e e e e e e e e!

And see the world the way you do.

Twinkle, twinkle, little star,
How I wonder what you are.

stairs,
the
climb
time to
When it's

24

To brush my teeth and say my prayers,

Through my window I can see,

That you are smiling down on me.

Twinkle, twinkle, little star, How I wonder what you are,

There's so much more I'd like to say,

Maybe we'll talk another day.